**Discovering
Cultures**

Sweden

Deborah Grahame

Marshall Cavendish
Benchmark
New York

*For Sara Nilsson, my fourth-grade friend in Sweden who provided valuable information
about school and other pastimes in her native land*

With thanks to Susan Brantly, Professor of Scandinavian Studies, University of Wisconsin at Madison,
for the careful review of this manuscript.

Marshall Cavendish
99 White Plains Road
Tarrytown, New York 10591-9001
www.marshallcavendish.us

Text copyright © 2007 by Marshall Cavendish Corporation
Map and illustrations copyright © 2007 by Marshall Cavendish Corporation

Library of Congress Cataloging-in-Publication Data

Grahame, Deborah A.
Sweden / by Deborah Grahame.
p. cm. — (Discovering cultures)
Includes bibliographical references and index.
ISBN-13: 978-0-7614-1985-3
ISBN-10: 0-7614-1985-3
1. Sweden—Juvenile literature. I. Title. II. Series.
DL609.G73 2006
948.5—dc22   2006011474

Photo Research by Candlepants Incorporated
Cover Photo: SuperStock/age fotostock

The photographs in this book are used by permission and through the courtesy of; *SuperStock*: age fotostock, 1, 4, 22, 28, 29,
31, 34, 43(lower right); Silvio Fiore, 27. *Getty Images*: Johner Images: 6, 12(left), 32; Ullamaija Hanninen, 9; 44(top left), 44(lower
right), 45. *Corbis*: Bob Krist, 7, 16(right), 42(lower right); Bo Zaunders, 8, 15, 20; Ted Spiegel, 12(right); Macduff Everton, 13,
16(left), 43(top left); Reuters, 18; Chris Lisle, 26; Fabrizio Bensch/Reuters, 30; Robert Pratta/Reuters, 33; Staffan Widstrand, 35;
Stefan Lindblom, 37. *The Image Works*: Alex Farnsworth, 10, 17, 23, 25, Topham, 11, 19, 43(lower right) Hideo Hage/HAGA,
38; Masakatsu Yamazaki/HAGA, 39.

Cover: *Small ferries in winter, Stockholm, Sweden*; Title page: *Teenage boy*

Map and illustrations by Ian Warpole
Book design by Virginia Pope

Printed in Malaysia
1 3 5 6 4 2

Turn the Pages...

Where in the World Is Sweden?   4

What Makes Sweden Swedish?   10

Living in Sweden   16

School Days   22

Just for Fun   28

Let's Celebrate!   34

The Flag and Money   40

Count in Swedish   41

Glossary   41

Fast Facts   42

Proud to Be Swedish   44

Find Out More   46

Index   47

Where in the World Is Sweden?

Sweden is located on the continent of Europe. Sweden is a bit larger than the state of California in the United States. It is almost 1,000 miles (1,600 kilometers) long and nearly 300 miles (500 km) wide. Sweden is Europe's fifth largest country. Only Russia, Ukraine, France, and Spain are larger.

Sweden is in northern Europe in an area known as Scandinavia. Along with Norway, it is part of the Scandinavian Peninsula. Sweden is also part of the European Union (EU), a group of European countries that cooperate in matters of politics, money, and society.

Most of Sweden is covered with thick forests and many thousands of lakes and rivers. Woodlands cover about 70 percent of the country. Farmland covers only about 10 percent of the land. Forests and rivers are Sweden's most important natural resources. Rivers provide hydroelectric or water power, and forests provide lumber and paper products.

A river cuts through the snow in winter.

Map of Sweden

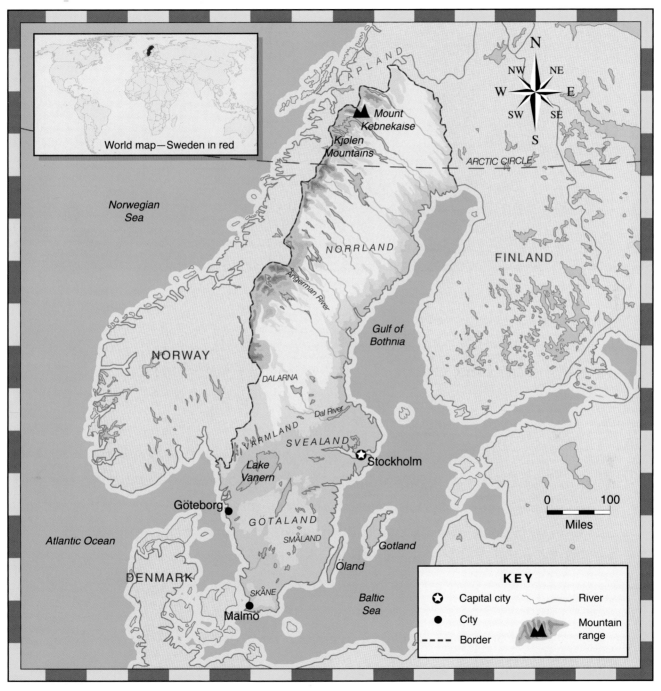

World map—Sweden in red

N
NW NE
W E
SW SE
S

LAPLAND

Mount Kebnekaise

Kjolen Mountains

ARCTIC CIRCLE

Norwegian Sea

NORRLAND

FINLAND

Ångerman River

Gulf of Bothnia

NORWAY

DALARNA

Dal River

VÄRMLAND

SVEALAND

Lake Vanern

Stockholm

Göteborg

GOTALAND

SMÅLAND

Gotland

Öland

Atlantic Ocean

DENMARK

SKÅNE

Malmö

Baltic Sea

0   100
Miles

KEY

★ Capital city		～ River	
● City		◣ Mountain range	
--- Border			

Mount Kebnekaise

Historically, Sweden was divided into four regions, called lands: Norrland, Svealand, Götaland, and Österland. In 1917, Österland became an independent country called Finland. Sweden is now divided into twenty-one counties, and the names of the three remaining lands are still widely used.

Norrland stretches across the north and takes up most of Sweden's land. Hills and pine forests cover this region. Most of the few people who live here make their home along the coast. Important rivers flow through Norrland, such as the Dal and the Ångerman. These rivers provide hydroelectric power for Sweden's industries, especially lumbering. Norrland is home to Mount Kebnekaise. At 6,926 feet (2,111 meters), it is Sweden's highest mountain. Mount Kebnekaise is part of the Kjølen Mountains. These mountains separate Sweden from Norway, its western neighbor. A region called Lapland covers the northern part of Norrland. Lapland crosses Norway and Finland into Russia.

An aerial view of Stockholm

Svealand means "land of the Swedes." The central provinces, including Värmland and Dalarna, make up this region of lakes, plains, and hills. Stockholm, Sweden's capital and largest city, is in the Svealand region on Sweden's east coast. In Stockholm, you will see churches that were built during the Middle Ages. This modern city also has a large subway system. Stockholm is built partly on mainland and partly on many small islands. Bridges connect one part of the city to another.

Two of Sweden's largest islands, Gotland and Öland, are part of Götaland. They lie to the east in the Baltic Sea. The land on these islands is different from the rest of the country. The soil is sandy and dry. The islands are used mostly for grazing farm animals. Many other groups of smaller islands are located along Sweden's long, rocky coastline.

Götaland is made up of highlands and lowlands. Most Swedes live in this region. Farmland makes up more than half of Götaland. The country's most *fertile* farmland is found in Skåne. Sugar beets, oats, and barley are grown here. Småland is north of Skåne, on the eastern coast of the Baltic Sea. Småland is the center of Sweden's glassworks industry. Sweden's major port cities, Malmö and Göteborg, are also in Götaland. Sweden's largest lake, Lake Vänern, at 2,156 square miles (5,584 sq km), crosses Svealand into Götaland.

The most northern part of Sweden lies in the Arctic Circle. Each year, here and in Lapland, there are seasons of endless day and endless night. The sun shines twenty-four hours a day for a period of six weeks, from mid-May to mid-July. In June and July, this region features "White Nights" when the sun never sets. For this reason, northern Sweden is known as the "Land of the Midnight Sun."

Wheat grows in a field in Skåne.

Reindeer

Reindeer live in Sweden and other northern areas of Europe and Asia. They make their home on the Arctic *tundra* and in forests and mountains. In North America, reindeer are called caribou.

In Sweden's Lapland, native people called the Sámi herd reindeer for a living. They use these mammals for milk, meat, clothing, and work. Male reindeer can grow antlers as long as 4.3 feet (1.3 m). Unlike other kinds of female deer, female reindeer have antlers, too.

Reindeer live well in the coldest parts of the world. They use their hooves and antlers to scrape under the snow in search of food. Reindeer do not eat meat, but they do eat grasses, shrubs, *lichens*, mushrooms, and roots. These foods are available throughout their habitat. One type of lichen, called reindeer moss, is the reindeer's favorite winter food.

What Makes Sweden Swedish?

Swedish girls smile for the camera.

Swedes are *descendants* of ancient people who lived in the area thousands of years ago. These people first came to Sweden when the glaciers melted, around 7,000–5,000 BCE.

Swedes speak Swedish. The Swedish and English languages both use the same alphabet, but Swedish has three extra vowels: Å, Ä, and Ö. Some Swedish and English words are similar, such as *hus* and house and *sommar* and summer. Today, English is Sweden's second language. All children are required to study it in school. Most adults speak it very well.

People from many countries live in Sweden. Like the United States, Sweden is a land of immigrants. After World War II, many people from other lands found jobs and safety in Sweden. By the early 1990s, about half a million immigrants were living in Sweden, many as guest workers. They came from Norway, Denmark, Iran, Turkey, Greece, and Chile. They entered Sweden to build a new life.

Sámi men in traditional dress with a reindeer

For almost 600 years, Finland was part of Sweden. Many Finns (people from Finland) live in Sweden today. Most have settled along the eastern coast and in the north. They are Sweden's largest minority group.

The Sámi have lived in Sweden longer than any other people. About 17,000 Sámi live in the northern regions, called Lapland. The Sámi have their own language and way of life. In the past they traveled with their reindeer herds to summer and winter pastures across the north. By the 1990s, most had settled in villages and towns. They work as miners and lumberjacks, as well as in business and government. The Sámi are known for their colorful *textiles* and handicrafts. They create beautifully carved knives and spoons from reindeer horn.

The *Vikings* were skilled at making beautiful objects from gold. Their work can still be seen in Swedish museums and in collections around the world. Today's Swedes also produce objects of beauty and fine design. Outdoors, graceful statues dot the countryside. Indoors, colorful murals decorate the walls of city buildings and subway platforms. Swedish glassware, ceramics, and furniture are

A gold Viking ring

Popular Swedish crafts include this painted wooden horse.

admired around the world. Ikea is a Swedish company popular today for its sturdy and simple furniture.

Over the centuries, a variety of music developed in Sweden. Swedish folk music dates back to the Middle Ages and is still popular today. During the 1800s, opera soprano Jenny Lind was known as the "Swedish Nightingale" because of her beautiful voice. During the 1970s, the Swedish pop group ABBA gave the international music scene such hits as "Dancing Queen."

A medieval cathedral on Gotland Island

Swedish literature is read and enjoyed throughout the world. August Strindberg wrote *Miss Julie* which is thought to be the greatest one-act play ever written. Selma Lagerlöf was the first woman and the first Swede to receive the Nobel Prize in Literature, in 1909. She wrote a popular children's story, *The Wonderful Adventures of Nils*, and other novels about Swedish country life.

In ancient times, Swedes worshipped gods such as Thor, Freya, and Odin. Then Sweden became a Christian country during the Middle Ages. For centuries from 1540 to 2000, all Swedes at birth became members of the Lutheran state church. But today, Sweden has no official church. Church and state are separate. People from many other countries who practice different religions now live in Sweden. About 14 percent of Sweden's population belong to other faiths, including Roman

Drottingholm Palace is home to Sweden's royal family.

Catholicism, Islam, and Judaism. Most Swedes do not go to church every Sunday. They do practice their faith for important family events, such as baptisms, weddings, and funerals.

Sweden's national government is a constitutional monarchy. This means the king or queen is the head of state, but performs only ceremonial duties. The prime minister heads the government and leads the cabinet of ministers. Sweden's *parliament* is called the *Riksdag*. Its 349 members are elected for four-year terms.

Skansen

Skansen is an outdoor folk museum near Stockholm. It is the largest museum of its kind in the world. This living museum looks the same today as it did when it was founded in 1891. There are 150 buildings where bakers, cobblers, and potters demonstrate their talents. Craftspeople in this unique place dress and work just as they did in Sweden long ago. These artists preserve the skills of the past as they make beautiful objects in wood, glass, lace, and iron.

Stockholmers gather at Skansen each New Year's Eve to listen to a poem, "Ring Out the Old, Ring in the New," by Alfred Lord Tennyson. This tradition began about one hundred winters ago.

Skansen attracts many art and history lovers and tourists, especially during the summer months.

Living in Sweden

Apartment buildings on a narrow road

Everyday life for Swedes means getting off to work and school on time, doing errands, and seeing family and friends. For part of the year it also means doing their best to be cheerful in the season of late morning sunrise and early afternoon sunset.

More than 9 million people live in Sweden. Most Swedes live and work in cities. They live in

Streets in Stockholm

large apartment complexes that have both indoor and outdoor playgrounds for winter and summer sports. Families with children also live in single- or two-family houses. Many Swedes in cities take trains, buses, and subways to go to work or to school. However, there are a lot of cars in Sweden. There is one car for every three people!

Just one hundred years ago, Sweden was a poor country. Most people were farmers or factory workers. Today Sweden is a wealthy nation with many industries and good jobs for its citizens.

Most jobs in Sweden are those that provide a service. These include jobs in education and health care, insurance, and personal services such as dry cleaning and hairstyling. Manufacturing jobs are also important. Ericsson is Sweden's major telecommunications company. It provides telephones and mobile phones for countries around the world. In fact, one of the earliest telephones was invented in Sweden.

Sweden manufactures Saab and Volvo automobiles and Electrolux appliances. *Ball bearings* were invented in Sweden and are still an important product. Sweden is the world's largest producer of safety matches. They were invented by a Swedish chemist in 1844. Iron ore is Sweden's most important

Working at the Ericsson mobile phone factory

mineral. The country also produces steel, lumber, and paper products. Sweden *exports* these goods around the world.

Swedes are concerned about their environment. They work hard to protect their land for future generations. One of the best paper-recycling programs has been developed in Sweden. Today, Sweden has nearly 1,500 national parks and protected wildlife areas.

Swedish men between the ages of eighteen and forty-seven must serve from seven to fifteen months in the armed forces. Swedish citizens can vote in national elections at age eighteen.

A person can become a Swedish citizen after living in the country for five years. But one can receive the benefits of Sweden's social and economic programs right away. These benefits include free hospital care, education, pensions for retired people, and child care. Taxes are high in Sweden. This helps the government pay for the programs. The country has expanded its social programs to help people from

A customer on a snowmobile picks up his meal at a McDonald's in northern Sweden.

other countries who come to live in Sweden. The government helps them learn the Swedish language, get an education, and find jobs.

Today, people from 166 nations make their home in Sweden. They have introduced ethnic foods into Swedish culture. Pizza shops, Chinese restaurants, and stalls offering Middle Eastern foods can be found along many Swedish streets. There is at least one McDonald's restaurant in every larger town.

When Swedes want information, they have more than 150 daily newspapers to choose from. They also enjoy watching television. Many programs are in English, and many are the same shows people in the United States watch. There is one big difference, however. The Swedish government does not allow commercials on TV or radio.

Swedish food is simple, hearty, and delicious. The sea provides Sweden's tables with many kinds of fish. Salmon, herring, trout, and mackerel are favorites. Fish dishes can appear at each meal. *Lutfisk* is codfish that is dried, and then boiled or baked. It has the texture of gelatin. But Swedes eat many other foods. Breakfast is often a roll, pastry, or cold cereal. Lunch may be an open-face

Freshly caught fish served with cucumbers and boiled potatoes

During Christmas, Swedes enjoy a smörgåsbord with family and friends.

sandwich on thin, dense bread. For dinner, Swedes like meatballs, stuffed cabbage, or ham. On Thursday nights, many families eat a thick pea soup with bits of pork, with pancakes for dessert. It is a weekly tradition followed by many restaurants, too.

The most famous Swedish food is actually a whole tableful of food—*smörgåsbord*, which means spread or sandwich table. But there are more than sandwiches at a smörgåsbord! There can be as many as one hundred different dishes on this table. People serve themselves, and they often eat the foods in a certain order. First there are fish dishes, cold dishes, hot dishes, a variety of breads, pounds of butter pats stacked into a pyramid, and finally, lots of desserts. Swedes serve smörgåsbord at home on special holidays such as Christmas and Easter.

Let's Eat!
Ingeborg's Plättar

These delicious Swedish pancakes are wafer-thin, but rich with eggs and milk.
Ask an adult to help you prepare them. Frying and flipping them is a bit tricky,
and takes practice! Wash your hands before you begin.

Ingredients:

3 eggs

2 cups whole milk

3/4 cup flour

1/8 teaspoon salt

1 to 2 tablespoons sugar

Pinch baking powder

2 tablespoons butter,
melted

Beat the eggs. Add milk. Then add the flour, salt, sugar, and
baking powder, mixing well. Stir in the melted butter last. (The less flour used,
the better. Add just enough to hold the batter together.)
Grease a round cast-iron skillet or griddle. Pour in enough batter to almost fill the
pan. When tiny bubbles appear on the surface of the pancake, flip carefully. Makes
ten pancakes. If you make these on a Thursday, serve them with pea
soup like they do in Sweden!

School Days

Swedish children between the ages of seven and sixteen must attend school. Tuition, lunches, school supplies, medical treatment, and books are all free during these years.

Grundskola is the Swedish name for elementary school. Students attend this school for nine years. Grades one, two, and three make up the lower grades of grundskola. The middle grades include fourth through sixth grade. The upper

Swedish schoolgirls with a younger child

grades are seventh through ninth grade. Students do not receive written grades for the first six years. Instead, teachers and parents meet at school conferences to discuss the student's progress. Students in eighth and ninth grades receive grades ranked on a scale of one to five (five is highest). No final exams are given.

During late fall through spring, children arrive at school before sunrise. Usually they walk or ride their bicycles. If school is too far, they ride the school bus. School uniforms are not common. Instead, children wear their own clothes. Throughout the day, children study the required subjects: Swedish, math, religion, history, geography, music, handicrafts, and gymnastics. Usually the class has just one teacher for all subjects.

A teacher assists her students.

In mid-morning or afternoon, students might have a snack of fruit brought from home. For lunch, children go to the cafeteria. They might have *pannbiff*, a kind of hamburger. They also eat spaghetti with meat sauce, fish and potatoes, grilled chicken, or pizza. Year-round, part of each school day is spent getting fresh air and exercise. After lunch and between classes, students take breaks to play soccer, known in Sweden as football.

If you visited a Swedish school, you would be able to speak some English with the students. This is because Swedish children begin to study English in fourth grade. They are required to study it until seventh grade. Most continue to study the language after that.

Preschool is common in Sweden, since many Swedish moms and dads work outside the home. Before they are ready for grundskola, children between the ages of eighteen months to six years can attend day care centers paid for by the government. Kindergarten is not required, but many children under seven years old attend a private school for this purpose. From ages seven to twelve, children can go to a "Leisure Time Center" while their parents work. The centers are open before and after school and during school vacations.

Children listen to a story at a Swedish day care center.

A scout uses a magnifying glass to examine tree bark.

After-school activities give children a chance to participate in their favorite sports and hobbies. They take dance or music lessons, play on the computer, and attend scout meetings. Neighborhood soccer games, skateboarding, and horseback riding are also pastimes they enjoy.

On the average, children have one hour of homework each night. After homework, children may watch television. Many programs are in English and other languages. They may also read books. Harry Potter books are popular in Sweden, as they are around the world.

In the seventh and eighth grades, children can choose some of their own subjects. Boys and girls alike must take courses in child care, home economics, and technology. In ninth grade, they choose one of nine courses of study. They may study art or another foreign language, such as French or German. After grundskola, students go on to secondary school. They can attend for up to three years. During that time, students must complete several weeks of work experience outside school. They prepare to learn job skills or to go to college.

The garden at Uppsala University

Sweden has six universities. The oldest is Uppsala University. It was founded in 1477. That's fifteen years before Christopher Columbus landed on America's shores! College tuition and even students' living expenses are free in Sweden.

Swedes value learning at all stages of life. Adults often attend classes in the evening after work. They usually study English or another foreign language. They might learn job skills. Adults who did not go to secondary school may finish their education this way. The classes are held in high schools and community centers.

Runes

Many centuries ago, Swedish people communicated with each other through writings using an alphabet called runes. Runes were symbols carved on stones and other hard surfaces such as wood. This sixteen-letter ancient alphabet has been found in parts of Sweden, Iceland, Britain, and northern Europe. Runes were carved on everything from road signs to personal messages. People carried small stones with runic carvings as good luck charms to protect them from disease or harm.

Just for Fun

People in Sweden enjoy being outdoors in *naturen* (nature), whatever the weather. Sweden's motto, "Sport for All," is certainly true. Swedes are an active, sports-loving people. They like to fish for salmon or trout, and hunt for deer or moose. Because the winter is so long, sports such as hockey, ice fishing, tobogganing, curling, ice skating, and skiing are popular during this season.

Throughout the year, sports can be enjoyed indoors or outdoors. Orienteering is a Swedish sport that has caught on in the United States. Participants are taken deep into the forest or countryside. They use compasses and maps to find their way back home. Tennis is also popular. Champion tennis players Björn Borg and Stefan Edberg inspired many young Swedes to take up the sport.

In general, winter months are devoted to work and summer is for play. All Swedes have five weeks of paid vacation from their jobs each year. In late

Fishermen using nets to catch herring

A family enjoys a day of sledding.

February, Swedes take a week-long winter break from work and school, usually called the ski vacation. Skiing in the snowy mountains is the main attraction for many Swedish families at this time. Other families travel to warm, sunny places, such as Spain, during the break.

In winter, Swedes can visit a theater sculpted completely of ice—even the stage props! Sweden's Ice Globe Theatre in Lapland is a copy of Shakespeare's Globe Theatre in London, England. It is a really "cool" place that is open from January through April. An ice hotel and an ice cinema stand nearby. In summer the structures melt away. Then, Lapland has another fun feature—midnight golf. Golfers can play on an all-night golf course in bright sunshine from midnight until it's time for breakfast!

Year-round, families like to see movies and go out for a meal together. They might also visit a museum. There are more than fifty museums in Stockholm alone!

Vasa, the ancient Swedish warship, on display in Stockholm

You can examine jewels and other treasures, or even the seventeenth-century battleship *Vasa*, once sunken on the ocean floor.

On weekends, Swedes might go to the mall for an afternoon of shopping. One of the first malls built in Stockholm is called Hötorget. It was built over an underground railway and is attached to five skyscrapers. Some shopping centers

Taking a dip in the lake

in other Swedish cities have rolling walkways, like the ones in many U.S. airports.

Stockholm and other cities seem deserted in July and August. This is because Swedes spend their summer vacation in the countryside. Here, wild strawberries, mushrooms, and lingonberries (like small, sweet cranberries) ripen for picking and eating. In the summer, families also enjoy camping, canoeing, kayaking, hiking, sailing, and swimming. They often make a yearly visit to an amusement park to ride the roller coaster or to splash in a water park.

Red summerhouses by the sea

Many Swedes own a *sommarstuga* (summerhouse) near a lake or by the sea. The islands surrounding Stockholm are full of these houses—about 600,000 of them! They are often painted dark red. The paint is red because it contains copper, which protects the house from severe weather.

Summer is also festival time, especially in the beautiful farmland of Dalarna in north central Sweden. Dalarna is known as the Folklore District. Folk music, dancing, and outdoor entertainment fill the meadows. Dancers and musicians wear traditional costumes. Tourists visit the area to view the folk art in the local shops.

Swedes on Skis

Swedes have been traveling on skis for centuries. The first skis were more than 9 feet long and 6 inches wide! Skiing began as a means of transportation many years before it was enjoyed as a sport. People long ago needed a way to get across deep snow during the long winters. Battles were fought by troops on skis during the late Middle Ages.

The world's biggest ski race, the Vasa Race, is held each March in Sweden. Ski jumping and slalom are popular pastimes in any community where there is a decent hill!

Let's Celebrate!

Sweden is a land of long, light days and long, dark nights. The country's holidays follow this pattern. Swedes celebrate the arrival of the light days of summer and dark nights of winter. They have great fun keeping these traditions alive.

Only about one hundred years ago, Sweden was mostly a country of farms. Seasonal festivals focused on planting and harvest times. They are still an important part of the Swedish year.

As springtime bursts across the land, Swedes celebrate Walpurgis Night. Bonfires blaze and people dance and sing on this last night of April. The holiday signals the coming of spring.

Walpurgis Night is celebrated with a bonfire in Stockholm.

A child waves a Swedish flag.

Easter is a three-day holiday. People observe Good Friday in a quiet way with special prayers and religious services. Families color eggs, and on Easter Saturday they eat some of them hard-boiled. On Easter Sunday, Swedes may attend church, and later have a special lamb dinner. Throughout this time, homes are decorated with *påskvippor*, which are brightly colored feathers attached to twigs and branches.

Halloween in the United States is a day for witches on broomsticks. In Sweden, children dress as witches on Easter Saturday. Long ago, the Swedes believed that at Easter, witches flew their brooms to the Blue Mountain to meet with the devil. The people lit firecrackers to scare the witches on their way. Today in some places, children dress in rags and wigs and carry pots and kettles for people to fill with coins.

Swedes celebrate Flag Day on June 6. During a special ceremony, the king and queen present the Swedish flag to groups and societies.

Swedes dressed for a Midsummer's Eve festival

Midsummer's Eve is one of the most colorful Swedish holidays. It occurs on the Friday between June 19 and 26. Swedes welcome summer to Sweden during this holiday. People decorate houses, churches, and other buildings with flowers. Swedes have picnics all day and dance around an enormous Maypole far into the night.

Crayfish season starts on the second Wednesday of August in Sweden. Crayfish look like miniature lobsters. They are known as crawfish in some parts of the U.S. Swedes cook and eat as many crayfish as they can, while wearing funny paper bibs and hats. Table manners are not required at this merry feast! Part of the fun is being messy and loud, surrounded by neighbors and friends.

On All Saints Day, November 1, Swedes place memorial flowers and plants on the graves of family and friends. The official holiday is observed on November 5. People remember other historic heroes in November. On the sixth they honor the memory of King Gustav Adolph, who died in battle during the 1600s. They remember the king with a special pastry shaped or decorated to look like him and served as a dessert or coffee break treat. Two Martins also have November remembrance days: religious leader Martin Luther on the tenth, and Saint Martin de Porres on the eleventh. It is the custom to serve roast goose with apples on both days.

An important date in Sweden is also noted around the world. Each year on December 10, the Nobel Prizes are awarded in a beautiful ceremony held at the Concert Hall in Stockholm. The Nobel Prizes are given to people who excelled in

The Nobel Prize award ceremony in Stockholm

physics, chemistry, medicine and physiology, literature, world peace, and economics. Along with this high honor, the winners receive a cash gift. The Nobel Peace Prize is awarded at a ceremony in Oslo, the capital of Norway.

Christmas is a time for family and traditions. There is a spirit of *gemenskap* (togetherness). On Christmas Eve, families share a meal of ham or fish. Small children wait for a visit from *Jultomten*, the Swedish name for the Christmas Elf or Santa Claus. After dinner, the family opens presents. At midnight, there is a special candlelit church service.

On New Year's Eve, fireworks, singing, and noisemaking fill the streets at midnight. Twelfth Night, January 6, is a public holiday. The brightly decorated Christmas tree stays in the home until Knut's Day on January 13. Friends arrive to take down the tree decorations while they nibble cake and cookies. After the party they toss the tree out into the snow!

Swedish Christmas decorations

Saint Lucia's Day

Children in Sweden especially enjoy Saint Lucia's Day, the Festival of Light, on December 13. This holiday marks the beginning of the Christmas season. Saint Lucia was a Christian saint. Her name means "light" in Latin.

Every child has a role to play on this holiday. The eldest daughter wakes long before dawn. She puts on a white dress and red sash. She carefully places a crown of candles or evergreens on her head. Her younger sisters are her maids. Brothers are star boys who wear cone-shaped hats decorated with stars. "Saint Lucia" brings her parents a tray of coffee, special breads, and ginger cookies. All day in schools and offices, people sing Lucia carols and serve traditional treats, such as Lucia Cats, a sort of saffron sweet roll decorated with raisins. The songs and sweets put people in a happy mood. The winter days may be dark, but the brightness of the holiday season has arrived!

The flag used by Sweden today was adopted in 1906. It has a yellow cross on a deep blue background. Other Scandinavian countries have similar cross designs, but in different color combinations. Why the cross? Most of these countries became Christian during the Middle Ages.

Sweden's form of money is the krona or crown. The krona comes in both paper bills and in coins called öre. One krona equals 100 öre. There is a 50 öre coin, as well as one for 1, 5, and 10 kronor (the plural for krona). The coins have designs from nature and from the Swedish coat of arms. Paper money has pictures of famous Swedes. The exchange rate changes often, but in 2006, 7.64 kronor equaled one U.S. dollar. Even though Sweden is a member of the European Union, it has not adopted the euro in place of the krona.

Count in Swedish

English	Swedish	Say it like this:
one	ett	ett
two	två	tvoh
three	tre	treh
four	fyra	FEE-ra
five	fem	fem
six	sex	sex
seven	sju	sheu
eight	åtta	AW-tah
nine	nio	NEE-oh
ten	tio	TEE-oh

Glossary

ball bearing   A part of a machine in which moving parts slide on rolling metal balls.

descendants (dee-SEN-duhnts)   People who come from a certain ancestor.

export   To ship goods to another country.

fertile (FURT-ul)   Able to produce crops; rich, productive.

lichens (LIE-kehns)   Moss-like plants that grow in patches on rocks and trees.

parliament (PAR-lih-ment)   The lawmaking part of the government of a country.

textile (TEKS-tile)   A woven or knitted fabric; cloth.

tundra (TUN-druh)   A large, flat plain without trees in the Arctic regions.

Vikings (VIE-kings)   Scandinavian pirates who raided the coasts of Europe during the eighth, ninth, and tenth centuries.

Fast Facts

Mount Kebnekaise
Kjølen Mountains
NORRLAND
Ångerman River
Gulf of Bothnia
DALARNA
Dal River
VÄRMLAND
SVEALAND
Lake Vanern
Stockholm
Göteborg
GÖTALAND
SMÅLAND
Gotland
Öland
SKÅNE
Malmö

Sweden is in northern Europe in an area known as Scandinavia. Along with Norway, it is part of the Scandinavian Peninsula. Sweden is also part of the European Union.

Sweden is almost 1,000 miles (1,600 km) long and nearly 300 miles (500 km) wide. It is Europe's fifth largest country.

Norrland is home to Mount Kebnekaise. At 6,926 feet (2,111 m), it is Sweden's highest mountain. Mount Kebnekaise is part of the Kjølen Mountains.

Stockholm, Sweden's capital and largest city, is in Svealand on Sweden's east coast. Stockholm is built partly on mainland and partly on many small islands.

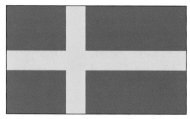

Sweden's flag has a yellow cross on a deep blue background. Other Scandinavian countries have similar cross designs, but in different color combinations.

In Sweden, 87 percent of the people are Lutheran and 13 percent are other religions, including Roman Catholic, Orthodox, Baptist, Muslim, Jewish, and Buddhist.

Sweden's form of money is the krona or crown. The krona comes in both paper bills and in coins called öre. One krona equals 100 öre. Even though Sweden is a member of the European Union, it has not adopted the euro in place of the krona.

Swedes speak Swedish. The Swedish and English languages both use the same alphabet, but Swedish has three extra vowels: Å, Ä, and Ö.

The Sámi have lived in Sweden longer than any other people. About 17,000 Sámi live in the northern regions, called Lapland.

Sweden's national government is a constitutional monarchy. This means the king or queen is the head of state, but performs only ceremonial duties. The prime minister heads the government and leads the cabinet of ministers.

As of July 2006, there were 9,016,596 people living in Sweden. Most Swedes live and work in cities.

Proud to Be Swedish

Astrid Lindgren (1907–2002)

Swedish author Astrid Lindgren invented a lively red-headed character, Pippi Longstocking, who has amused children for generations. This and other Lindgren titles have been translated into more than sixty languages. Astrid was raised on a small farm in Småland in southern Sweden. She loved to read as a child. Her favorite books included *Anne of Green Gables* and *Pollyanna*. After completing her education, she did office work, married, and had two children. She wrote and published children's stories during the 1930s and 1940s. In 1945, the first Pippi Longstocking book was published. The characters created by this well-loved author inspired a theme park out-side Stockholm and another in Finland.

Alfred Nobel (1833–1896)

Sweden's most successful businessman and inventor actually grew up in Russia. He was born in Stockholm and returned to Sweden with his parents when he was twenty. Nobel patented his most famous invention, dynamite, in 1867. The use of dynamite helped Sweden's mining indus-try to grow quickly. Nobel made a great fortune from this invention. He gave away large sums of money to people

in need during his lifetime. When he died, his will gave instructions for his $9 million fortune to be used for the creation of the Nobel Prizes. These are awarded each year for achievements in science, literature, medicine, world peace, and economics. The prizes are a high honor, and the winner receives a large sum of money. Swedish committees choose the winners. The Nobel Peace Prize is the most well known and respected of the Nobel Prizes. Unlike the other awards, its recipient is chosen by the Norwegian Parliament.

Raoul Wallenberg (1912–1947?)

One of the great heroes of World War II came from Sweden, even though Sweden did not fight in the war. Raoul Wallenberg, a Swedish diplomat, helped save thousands of Jews from the death camps. He worked with the United States and Swedish governments to get Swedish passports for Hungarian Jews. These documents made Jews instant Swedish citizens. They were allowed to live in safe houses set up by the Swedish government in Hungary. Wallenberg also got food and medical supplies through to these houses. When Russia invaded Hungary, Wallenberg was arrested and never heard from again. It is believed that he died in prison shortly after the war. The United States, Canada, and Israel made Wallenberg an honorary citizen of their countries. Sweden has also honored him with a special postage stamp.

Find Out More

Books

The Sami of Northern Europe (First Peoples) by Deborah Robinson. Lerner Publications, Minnesota, 2002.

Sweden by Tracey Boraas. Capstone Press, Minnesota, 2003.

Welcome to My Country: Welcome to Sweden by Vimala Alexander and Michelle Wagner. Gareth Stevens Publishing, Wisconsin, 2003.

You Wouldn't Want to Be a Viking Explorer! (Voyages You'd Rather Not Make) by Andrew Langley. Franklin Watts, New York, 2001.

Web Sites*

www.astridlindgrensworld.com
Read about the author's life, her popular children's book characters, and the hands-on museum and theme parks that are dedicated to her work.

www.smorgasbord.se/
Learn about Nordic gods, Vikings, and how to trace your Swedish roots.

Videos

Families of the World: Families of Sweden. Master Communications, Inc., 1998.
See what it's like to visit and live with two Swedish families, from breakfast to bedtime.

*All Internet sites were available and accurate when sent to press.

Index

Page numbers for illustrations are in **boldface.**

maps, 5, 42

amusement parks, 31, 44
animals, 9, **9**, **11**
architecture, 7, 11, **13**, **14**, 17, **26**, 29, 30, 32, **32**
art, 11, 32

cities, 8, 16, 30–31, 43
    capital, 7, **7**, 15, **16**, 29–30, 42
citizenship, 18, 22
clothing, **11**, 15, **15**, 22, 32, 35, **36**, 39
coastline, 7
crafts, 11, **12**, 15

day care centers, 18, 24, **24**
days and nights, 8, 22, 29, 34, **34**, 36, **36**, 39, **39**

economy, 17
education, 10, 18, 22–26, **23**, **24**, **25**, **26**, 28
elderly people, 18
environmental concern, 18
ethnic groups, 9, 11, **11**, 19, 43
    See also immigrants

farming, 4, 7–8, **8**, **15**, 17, 34
Finland, 6, 11
flag, 35, **35**, 40, **40**, **42**
food, **18**, **19**, 19–20, **20**, 23, 31, 35, 36, 37, 39
    recipe, 21
forests, 4, 6, 28

good luck charms, 27, **27**
government, 14, 18–19, 24, 35, 43
    in World War II, 45

health care, 18
heroes, 37, 45
history, 6, 11, 27, 37
    ancient times, 10, 11, 13, 27, **27**, **30**
    reenactments, 15, **15**
holidays and festivals, 15, 20, **20**, 32, **34**, 34–39, **35**, **36**, **38**, **39**
houses, **16**, 16–17, 32, **32**, 35

ice sculpture, 29
immigrants, 10, 18–19
inventions, 17, 44
islands, 7, 32

jobs, 9, 11, 15, 17, **17**, 19, 25, 28

lakes and seas, 8, **31**
landscape, 4, **4**, 6, 7, 9
languages, 10, 11, 19, 23, 43
    counting, 41
    runes, 27, **27**
Lapland, 6, 9, 11, 29
leisure, 23, 25, **28**, 28–31, **29**, **31**, 33, **33**
Lindgren, Astrid, 44, **44**
literature, 13, 44
location, 4, **5**, 8, 42

mining, 17, 44
money, 40, **40**, 43
mountains, **5**, 6, **6**, 42
museums, 15, **15**, 29–30, **30**
music, 12, 32

neighboring countries, 4, **5**, 6
newspapers, 19
Nobel, Alfred, **44**, 44–45

Nobel Prizes, **37**, 37–38, 45
    winner, 13
northern region, 6, 8, 9, 11, 32

Pippi Longstocking, 44
playgrounds, 17
population data, 7, 10, 13, 16, 43
products, 4, 6, 8, 11–12, 17–18

regions, 6–7
religion, 7, **13**, 13–14, 35, 37, 38, 39, 43
rivers, 4, **4**, 6
rural life, 13, 15, **15**, 31, 32

Scandinavia, 4, 42
seasons, 8, 22, **28**, 28–29, **29**, 31, **31**, 32, **32**, 34, **34**, 36, **36**, 39, **39**
shopping, 30–31
singers, 12
size, 4, 42
sports, 23, 25, 28, 29, **29**, 31, 33, **33**
statues, 11

taxes, 18
theaters, 29, **37**
tourist sites, 15, **15**
transportation, 7, 11, 17, **18**, 22, **30**, 30–31, 33, **33**

vacations, 28–29, **31**, 31–32, **32**
Vikings, 11

Wallenberg, Raoul, 45, **45**
warfare, 18, 33
women, 13
World War II, 45

About the Author

After working as a book editor and reviewer for many years, Deborah Grahame writes children's books from her Connecticut home. Deborah's Baltic roots give her a special affinity for that region's Scandinavian neighbors. She has fond childhood memories of herring in cream sauce, pancakes, and strong, sweet coffee served in her Nana's upstairs kitchen.

Acknowledgments

Special thanks go to Maisi Summ, a new Swedish friend who read the final manuscript and helped along the way.